THE ADVENTURES OF PIPÌ
THE PINK MONKEY

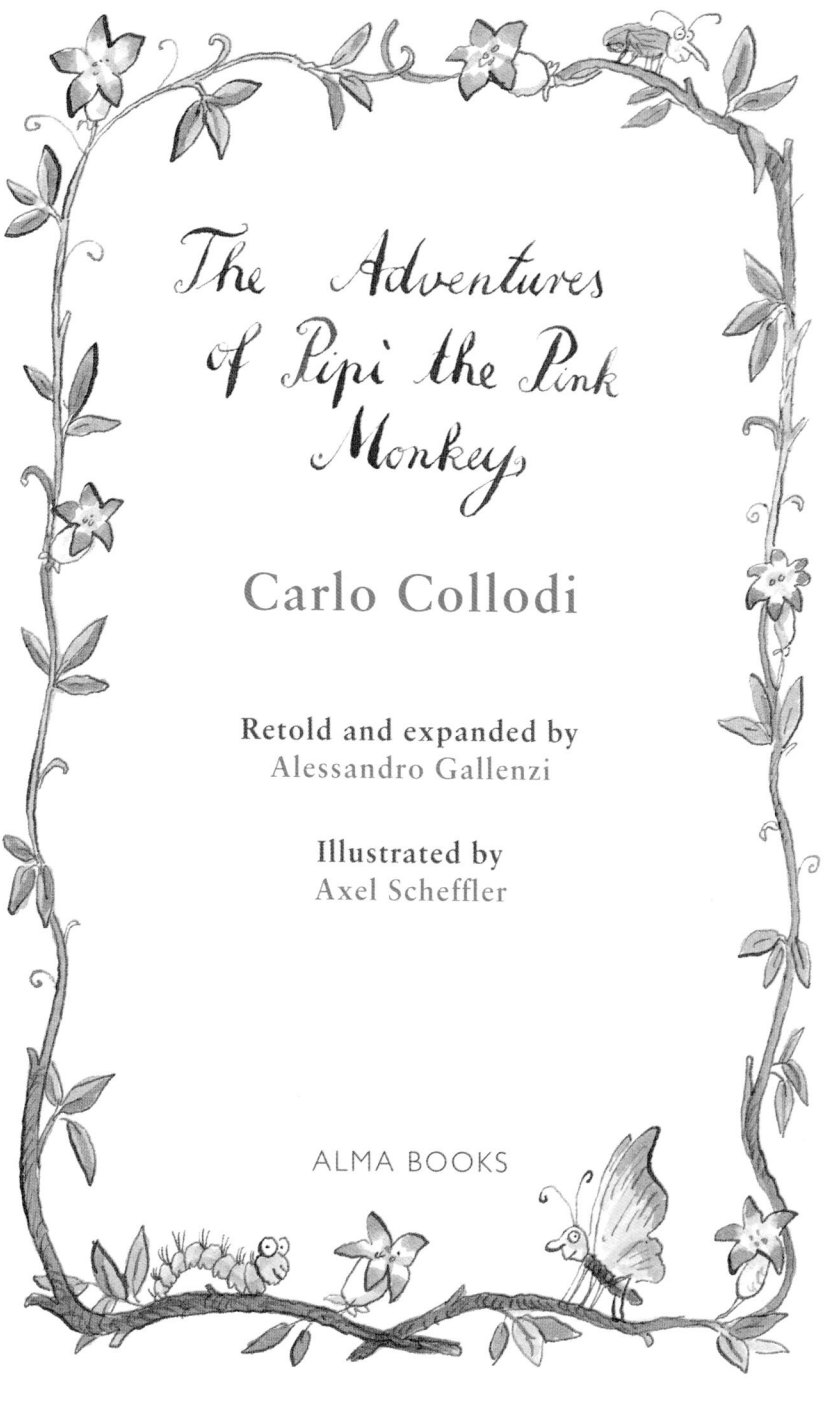

The Adventures of Pipì the Pink Monkey

Carlo Collodi

Retold and expanded by
Alessandro Gallenzi

Illustrated by
Axel Scheffler

ALMA BOOKS

ALMA CLASSICS LTD
3 Castle Yard
Richmond
Surrey TW10 6TF
United Kingdom
www.almaclassics.com
www.almajunior.com

First published by Alma Classics Ltd in 2016

Text and Extra Material © Alessandro Gallenzi, 2016
Inside and cover illustrations © Axel Scheffler

Printed and bound by Oriental Press Dubai

ISBN: 978-1-84749-559-4

CONTENTS

The Adventures of
Pipì the Pink Monkey

ONCE UPON A TIME, in the famous land of Hullabaloo, there lived a small family of monkeys: mum, dad and five little ones, all boys, who were knee-high to a grasshopper. The family lived among the branches of a giant tree in the middle of a forest, paying fifteen plums a year in rent to an arrogant old gorilla who claimed to be the landlord.

Of the five little monkeys, four had dark, chocolate-coloured fur, while the youngest – from who knows what freak of nature – was covered with a fine pink down, similar to the petals of a rose in May. And this is why everyone, both at home and out in the forest, nicknamed him Pipì, which in monkey language means exactly that: "coloured like a rose".

Pipì didn't look like his brothers or the other young monkeys living around their tree, and not just because he was pink. He had a lively, intelligent face, mischievous bright eyes that kept darting about, a smiling little mouth and a lean, wiry body, flexible as a riding crop. He was, if truth be told, a really handsome little chap.

Seeing him gambol around and hearing the racket he made, an observer might have mistaken Pipì for an eight- or nine-year-old boy: like a boy he chased butterflies and went nest-hunting; like a boy he chomped all the time on anything he could find, greedy for unripe fruit; and like a boy – a boy with no manners – he'd wipe his mouth with the back of his hand after stuffing himself with food, before studiously licking his fingers one by one.

But Pipì's greatest passion was to copy humans and everything they did. One hot day in summer, as he wandered about the forest hunting for crickets, cicadas and other insects, he saw an old man sitting at the foot of a tree with a pipe sticking out of his mouth. Pipì was spellbound.

"Oh," he said to himself, "I wish I could have that smoking twig! My brothers would die of envy to see me puffing out clouds of smoke from my mouth like him!"

The afternoon sun was strong, and the heat was unbearable. After a while, the old man yawned, placed his smouldering pipe on the grass and dozed off. Moving gingerly, Pipì climbed down the trunk of the tree. Holding his breath, he stretched out his arm, little by little, then snatched the pipe and bolted away just as the man woke up and shouted at him to stop.

Back in his treetop home, he called out to his brothers and showed them how he could blow smoke out of his mouth. Pandemonium broke out all along the branches. Dodò, his older brother, wanted to try the pipe too and snatched it from Pipì, while the other siblings jumped and laughed and shrieked with excitement. Babà, one of the smaller monkeys, fell out of the tree and had to limp back up, bawling his head off, more out of disappointment than pain.

Alarmed by the commotion, Pipì's mum and dad rushed to see what was happening. They found Gugù and Memè fighting over the pipe, and Dodò coughing and spluttering on the grey billows of smoke coming out of his mouth and nose.

Pipì's dad shook his head. "Whose idea was this?"

Four brown fingers pointed at the little pink monkey.

"It was Pipì's," said Babà, still tearful. "He stole the smoking wood from a man in the forest."

Their dad shook his head again. "You should not steal, Pipì," he said with a gentle voice, "and you should not smoke. You must remember that every action has its own consequences: if you steal today, you may come to a bad end tomorrow. And smoking may seem fun now, but it may harm you in the future. You should not copy what men do: one day you'll grow up and understand this, son. But if you are not careful now, it may be too late then."

"Sorry, Dad," Pipì said, stifling a naughty smile. Being daddy's favourite, he knew he could get away with all sort of mischief, risking at worst a few words of reproach. "I won't do it again," he added, looking up with eyes that said the exact opposite.

"Very well," said Pipì's dad, prising the pipe from Memè's grasp, who let go with a rueful whine. "Now let me tell you a story." Beckoning, he invited his wife to sit next to him. The five little monkeys eagerly jumped onto a branch opposite him, arranged themselves from tallest to shortest, with Pipì right at the end of a leafy branch. "It's about a human – a man who lived to regret one single action he did when he was younger."

"Who is he? Who is he?" shouted the little monkeys, who always listened with delight to their dad's stories.

"His name is Ticklythroat," he said. "But he wasn't always called that. When he was young, he used to be a very handsome boy, just like you lot are handsome little monkeys, but then…"

"Then what? Then what? Tell us, Dad."

"Then, as I said, he did something wrong. He didn't deliver on a promise he had made – and so he was punished for it."

"What happened, Dad?" shouted Babà.

"He was in love with a beautiful girl called Bella. They were soon to be married, and he had promised to bring her some turquoise flowers for her wedding dress. He was picking them in the forest when he saw an old man sitting at the foot of a tree, smoking on a *glup-glup* – yes, just like this one." Dad waved the pipe around and stared at Pipì, who looked away. "Ticklythroat had never seen a *glup-glup* before, and wanted to try it out, so he stole it from the man and ran away. The thing is, he didn't know the man was a wizard... and that the *glup-glup* was a magic one."

"Oh," said Gugù.

"As soon as he started puffing away as he went on his way, he realized something was wrong. The smoke grew to envelop him like a thick fog, and he no longer knew where he was going. So he got lost in the forest and wandered around, unable to find a way out. The only thing he could see was his own shadow, which kept stretching and shrinking as days – yes, days – passed. At least, he *thought* they were days: in fact they were *years*. After a terrible passage of time, after endless meanderings, he met the old man again. 'Here's your smoking wood,' he said, sobbing. 'Now break your spell and let me go, I beg you!' The old man looked him in the eyes. He saw that the boy had no malice and was good at heart. He also saw that he was sorry and had learnt his lesson. So the old man lifted the spell and set him free."

"And then?" said Memè.

7

"Then Ticklythroat ran home as fast as lightning, desperate to see Bella. But as soon as he was out of the forest, he noticed that something had changed. Where there used to be a cornfield, now there was a cottage with a garden; where the ferry used to take him across the river, now there was a large stone bridge. The people he met were wearing strange clothes and hats he had never seen before, and when he asked for directions, they didn't understand him and answered in a language he didn't know. Eventually he reached the place where Bella's house used to be, and he gasped – it was a ruin. He pulled at his hair and shuddered – centuries had passed since he'd left to pick turquoise flowers for her wedding dress, and the fairies had long taken her away."

"So they didn't marry in the end?" gulped Gugù.

Pipì's dad shook his head.

"What a sad story," said Memè. "All for a stupid stolen piece of wood."

"And a broken promise," added Dodò.

"What happened to Ticklythroat?" asked Pipì in a squeaky voice.

His dad fixed his stare on him. "He continues to live his miserable life outside the forest. He's a very angry man now, and he's turned into a brigand. He and his gang of thieves – the Swooping Magpies, people call them – are the terror of the land."

"Do they rob people?" said Babà.

"Yes, they do, dear," Mum suddenly piped in. "They rob, beat, kidnap – and even kill strangers."

"This is why you should never set foot outside the forest," said Pipì's dad. "It's very dangerous. Understood, boys?"

The five little monkeys nodded.

"Now, will you take this back to its owner, Pipì?"

"Sure, Dad," the little pink monkey said, earnestly, but curling his mouth into a smile when he looked away. "I'll do it – I'll do it straight away."

He grabbed the pipe and with a few agile jumps disappeared from view, to find a place where he could hide it and smoke some more another day without being disturbed.

2.

THE NEXT MORNING, at the break of dawn, Pipì was already scampering around the edges of the forest, looking for the best way to leave the trees behind. His head was still foggy and his throat burned from the previous day's smoking, but he was a very curious little monkey, and no blankets of smoke, no ticklish throats or swooping magpie-robbers could stop him from exploring the dangerous world beyond his homely trees.

A path on the west side of the forest led him around the shores of a vast lake. According to stories he had heard from his parents, this was the haunt of Snapper, a ridiculously old crocodile who had become blind with age. Two thousand years old, that's how old Snapper was said to be, and since he could no longer hunt for food, he squatted near the shore with his head above water and his jaws open wide, hoping that something juicy would fall into his mouth, or that a passer-by would give him some food, something chewable that would enable him to get by for another thousand years or so. But rather than throwing him a fish, some fruit or even a rotten vegetable, people taunted him: a handful of stones were thrown into his mouth, a bunch of nettles or brambles, a rusty nail or harpoon, or any old junk found on the road. Snapper would never get angry at these pranks, but just spat out the stones, the nettles, the brambles and the nails, and give a slight shake of his big, craggy head, as if to say: "One day…"

As he turned a bend in the path, Pipì saw a massive, jagged "V" sticking out from the lake's surface.

"There he is!" he said to himself, jumping with excitement. "Let's see if it's true that Snapper never snaps!"

He went over to the old crocodile and, standing at a safe distance on the shore, called to him.

"Good day, Mr Croc."

"Good day to you," Snapper said.

"Can you hear a rumbling noise? There must be rain on the way."

"It's my stomach."

"Are you hungry, Mr Croc?"

"I'm very hungry."

"Oh, I see. And what would you like to eat? Meat? Fruit?"

"Anything you want to give me."

"But would you rather have meat or fruit?"

"It's not for an old, blind, starving crocodile to choose. Whatever you give me, I'll take it."

"All I have around me is sand, cobwebs and hot air. How does that take your fancy, Mr Croc?"

Snapper gave a slight shake of his head and remained silent.

Soon Pipì was conjuring up imaginary meals in delicious detail, describing the irresistible aromas of roasted meat, the juiciness of ripe melons and the succulence of fresh fish, but the ancient crocodile showed no sign of annoyance other than the growing grumbling of his belly. The only thing that seemed to bother him was when a fly or a wasp came to rest on the tip of his nose: he would then jerk his head and shake it until the insect buzzed away.

"You'll need to be patient, Mr Croc," said Pipì, "and wait for someone with tastier food than mine."

"Old creatures are always patient," said Snapper, "especially with the young ones."

"Oh well. I must be on my way now, Mr Croc. Good luck with your peckishness!"

But before leaving, Pipì couldn't resist playing one last piece of mischief. He stole onto a bough that was hanging over the lake and crept from branch to branch until he was right above Snapper's jaws. Then he lowered his tail and started tickling the tip of the crocodile's nose, imitating a fly landing just above Snapper's left nostril. It was true that Snapper was blind, but he had not lost his hearing or his sharp sense of smell, so as soon as he felt the brush of Pipì's tail on his nostrils – whoosh! – he sprang up like a youthful croc and – snap! – bit it clean off.

Pipì let out a dreadful monkeyish cry of agony and, jumping off the tree, screeching, scarpered at full speed back towards the forest.

"Thank you, kind traveller," Snapper called after him, chewing on Pipì's tail. "There'll be no more rumbling for today."

Pipì ran and ran until he reached the edge of the forest, where he stopped and found enough courage to turn and look down his back. His tail – his lovely, fluffy, pink tail – was no more. That nasty old scoundrel of a crocodile had bitten it off, chewed it into bits and swallowed it down into his horrible stomach. The ugly red stump throbbed with waves of pain. Should he go back home and get the wound treated by his mum? But what would his dad say? This time Pipì wouldn't get away with a few gentle words of reproach. And what about his brothers and friends? They'd mock him for the rest of his life! Who wouldn't laugh at a monkey with no tail?

Ashamed, disconsolate and smarting, Pipì wandered aimlessly around the forest for hours and hours, until the shadows of the night descended from the top of the trees, wrapping him in gloom. Not able to bring himself to return to his family, he found a quiet spot where he could rest for the night. He lay on a heap of twigs covered with leaves and closed his eyes to sleep, but just as he was about to drift off, he heard an angry voice crying out:

"Ah, so who have we here!"

Pipì opened his eyes and saw a lantern lighting up an angry face – it was the old man he'd met in the forest the day before.

"Where is my pipe, little pink monkey?" the man demanded. "Give it back!"

Pipì tried to say that he had left the *glug-glug* in the secret cavity of an old tree trunk near his home, but what came out was only a frightened mumbling noise. He leapt up and made to escape, but the man grabbed him and shoved him in a large sack, tying it shut with a knot.

"Let me out! Let me out!" Pipì cried. "I'll go and fetch your smoking twig, I promise!"

But the man didn't hear him and, throwing the sack over his shoulder, he stomped off across the forest, muttering.

"This'll teach you a lesson, you horrible little monkey."

After a long walk, the old man stopped and tied the sack astride the rump of some large four-legged animal. There was a slap and a whistle, and the beast sped off into the night, carrying away the unfortunate Pipì on its back.

CONFINED IN THE DARKNESS of the sack, constantly jolted here and there, Pipì lost all sense of time – did his journey last for hours or entire days? Every now and then he shouted for help, but there was never a reply. Was there a rider, he wondered, or was the beast that was taking him farther and farther away unmounted? What kind of animal would run for hours or days at a stretch without stopping? A horse? Or something more dangerous – a tiger, a leopard? If it was a big cat, surely he'd end up eaten. In such confused thoughts he spent most of his time, with pangs of fear and guilt troubling his little heart.

In the end, Pipì's exhaustion was such that he could no longer hear any clomping or feel any jostling, and the darkness gave way to a colourful vision. No longer in a sack, he was travelling on the back of a winged animal – half horse, half eagle – that was flying in wide circles towards the moon. They landed among sky-high trees loaded down with the juiciest peaches and shiniest plums ever seen, indescribably better than the ones that grow on earth. Wherever he looked, he could see mountains of sugar, lakes of honey and rivers of milk, with copses of chestnut trees and cherry trees scattered around. He advanced through a field of *dop-dops* – the name monkeys give to candy canes. Some of them were white, some striped with red, others entirely pink, just like his tail. That's when it came to him – if he searched hard enough, perhaps he could find his tail here! Then he could go back to his family without shame.

And as Pipì made his way through the sugary sticks… look, there it is! – his beloved tail, which Snapper had cruelly bitten off – over there, only a short distance away. Burning with joy, he sprang forward and reached out to grab it, but a fluffy rabbit with turquoise fur popped up from nowhere to stop him.

"What do you think you're doing, little monkey?"

"It's mine!" Pipì shouted, angry and disappointed. "It's my tail!"

"I'm afraid you lost it," the rabbit said.

"Can't I get it back now that I've found it?"

The rabbit gave him a thoughtful look. "Maybe," she said. "But not now."

"When, then?"

"After you stop telling lies – and after you fulfil your promise."

"Which promise?"

"You'll find out."

He wanted to ask the rabbit more questions, but a great stomping noise behind him had him turning round to see the towering figure of a giant, billowing smoke from a pipe in his mouth.

"He's still furious with you," said the rabbit. "Quick, run!"

Pipì fled, but it was difficult to run among the candy canes, and he kept bumping into them and knocking them to the ground or breaking them. Behind him the giant's steps were getting nearer, and the obnoxious smell of smoke was spreading all around, making it hard for him to see where he was putting his feet. As he was looking for his flying steed, his eagle-horse, he tumbled headfirst into one of the honey lakes. He tried to swim, but the honey was so sticky that he couldn't make any progress. With great effort he dragged himself out of the lake and made it towards a tree, looking for shelter. As he started clambering up, he realized that his hands and body were still sticky and he could not move – and now the huge great hairy mitt of the giant was sweeping in to catch him.

His scream, as he awoke from this nightmare, was drowned by an even louder cry, perhaps the bray of a donkey or the neigh of a horse. The sack in which he was tied fell to the ground, and Pipì heard the retreating clop of the beast that had carried him. He lay there a moment, panting, listening, then tried to claw and gnash his way out, but all his efforts were in vain: the cloth of the sack was too tough and densely woven. Frightened, exhausted, starving, Pipì started crying – a soft, whiny cry mingled with broken words: "My tail… I'll never… oh, Daddy… oh, Mummy… I…"

Just then he heard a little squeaky voice.

"Are you OK in there?"

Pipì stopped weeping and crouched inside the sack, half in fear, half in hope. "Who are you?" he asked.

"I'm a mouse, and my name's Nibbler. I was crossing the road when that stupid horse reared in fright and knocked you off its back."

"Oh, Nibbler, I'm all right – only a few scratches, perhaps. My name's Pipì, and I'm a young monkey. An evil man chucked me in this sack and tied the top with a knot. Would you mind helping me out?"

"Let me see," Nibbler squeaked. He tried gnawing at the sack with all his strength, but the cloth didn't yield. He sighed and said: "Mmm, this won't be easy."

"Why?"

"The fabric seems tougher than leather. It would take me three months to nibble a hole."

"Three months?" cried Pipì. "I'll be dead by then, Nibbler! You'll only find a small heap of fur and a bundle of bones inside! Is there anything else you can do?"

"What can a little mouse do, Pipì? I am sorry, but I can't see how I can get you out."

"Where are we? Is there anyone else around?"

"We are at the top of a hill, in the open countryside. Hang on, I can see a billy goat over there. Give me a moment: I'll go and talk to him. He's much stronger than me. Perhaps he can help."

Nibbler returned a few minutes later with the goat, who was called Basher.

"So you can't get out?" Basher said.

"The cloth's so tough," said Pipì, "I can't rip it open."

"Leave it with me: let me have a go," said the goat. "I'll give it one of my almighty head-butts and crack it like a dry leaf, you'll see."

Basher lowered his head, took a long run-up and knocked the sack – with Pipì inside it – for all he was worth, sending it flying into the air a yard or two, before it started rolling down the hill.

Pipì shrieked in agony at the blow, letting out a new cry at each tumble: "Oh, poor me!" – "Oh, help!" – "Oh, I'm dying!"

Basher and Nibbler ran after the sack at top speed, unable to catch up with it. In the end, it rolled to a halt on the lawn of an elegant country house whose façade was almost entirely covered with ivy. The goat and the mouse stepped cautiously towards the sack to check if Pipì was alive or dead, but just as they reached it they saw a huge Newfoundland dog bounding in their direction, barking.

"Run, Basher, run!" cried the mouse. "You jump a fence, I'll find a hole to scurry down. Pipì," he yelled, darting away, "I'm sorry we couldn't help you. I hope you can get out of there. Good luck!"

And before the dog could snap at him, Nibbler dashed behind a bush and disappeared.

4.

"W HAT HAVE WE GOT there then, Soot?" said a man as the dog kept sniffing and snuffling at the folds of the sack. "Mmm," he added, scratching his bald head, "this old thing must have been dropped by the post coach, or by some drunken traveller. Let's take it inside and show it to Master Alfred, shall we?"

Holding the sack in his arms, the man walked into the house, followed by the tail-wagging Soot. He stepped into a large drawing room on the ground floor, where a blond-haired boy of around ten was having his breakfast.

"What's that, George?" the boy said, raising an eyebrow.

"I don't know, Master Alfred," the man said. "I've just found it on the lawn. Someone either threw it away or lost it."

"Will you open it?"

"If you wish."

George placed the sack on the floor and untied the knot, while Soot circled around, whimpering with impatience. When the contents of the sack were finally uncovered, Alfred clapped his hands and beamed.

"My monkey!" he exclaimed. "My pet monkey!"

The butler gave him a puzzled look. "Which monkey, sir?"

"The one I asked for – it's my birthday present. The one I want to take with me on board the ship when I go and visit Mum and Dad."

"But your birthday is not for another six months, Master Alfred."

"Well, does it matter, George? I'm so happy! A beautiful pink monkey! The Fairy has heard my prayers… Oh!" The boy frowned. "It's got no tail!"

"Maybe it just fell off."

"Let's see." Alfred crouched down and searched the sack for the missing tail. As his hand brushed against Pipì's back, the little monkey gave a slight twitch. At that, Soot, startled, burst into furious barking. Pipì jumped up on his back legs, throwing anxious looks around. As he saw the big gaping jaws of the Newfoundland loom over him, he thought he was soon going to be the big hound's dinner. With one bound he sprang onto the chandelier above and started jumping from one arm to another, making it swing like a crazy pendulum.

"Get down! Get down!" shouted George, fearing for the safety of the precious crystalware, while Soot barked as if possessed.

Alfred laughed his head off to see the effect of Pipì's overhead frolics on his butler's face. Realizing that the monkey would never come down as long as there was a huge black dog baying at him, he gestured to George.

"Better take Soot out of the room, George," he said. "I'd like to have a private conversation with our visitor. Please close the door behind you."

The butler bowed and went out of the room, dragging the reluctant Soot by the scruff of the neck.

Alone, Alfred and Pipì stared at each other for a very long time, silent and unmoving. In the end, Pipì's naughty expression – the sly curl of his lips, the roguish twinkle of his eye – got the better of Alfred's powers of self-control, and the boy burst into a fit of laughter, followed by the monkey's cheerful screech.

"Do you understand me?" Alfred asked, still giggling.

Pipì smiled and nodded.

"What's your name?"

"Pipì."

"Oh, so you can speak?"

Pipì nodded again.

"Very well. That will be our secret. Where is your family?"

"I have no family."

"How old are you?"

"I'm the youngest of five brothers."

"And how old are they?"

"They're younger than Mum and Dad."

"You said you had no family."

"I have a very short memory."

"All right, I understand what kind of mischief-maker you are," Alfred said, laughing. "And where did you lose your tail?"

"I don't know."

"What do you mean, 'You don't know'?"

"I must have lost it on the way. I don't remember. I told you I have a very short memory."

"Are you sure you're not telling a lie?"

"I never lie."

"You never lie? Are you sure?"

"Well, all right, sometimes I do lie – but only if I'm ashamed of saying the truth."

"So tell me the truth: did you run away from home?"

"I didn't run away. Someone put me in a sack and I was carried away."

"What are you going to do now?"

"I don't know. I'm sure I'll think of something. I need very little to be happy."

"Such as?"

"Well, you know… eating, drinking, having a bit of fun… I don't ask for more."

"You're a very decent monkey. But who's going to feed you?"

Pipì cast him a smiling glance. "You, perhaps?"

Alfred gave this some thought. "Mmm," he finally said. "Why not?" There was a pause. "I'll tell you what we are going to do: I'm prepared to feed you – but on the condition that you earn your keep. How about that? Are you used to working?"

"To be honest," Pipì said, "I'm more used to watching other people work. It's much more fun."

"Would you like to work as my valet?"

"Of course I would!"

"In a few days," said the boy, becoming serious, "I'll be leaving on a long journey. Would you like to be my valet and my travelling companion, sharing all the adventures with me?"

"Of course I would!"

"Every morning, for breakfast, I'll give you five pears, five apricots and a crunchy piece of fresh bread. Do you like fresh bread?"

"Of course I do!"

"Then you'll have lunch with me, and eat a large dish of peaches, plums and apricots. You like apricots, right?"

"Of course I do!"

"And for dinner you'll have eight walnuts and four figs: you have no problem with that, I suppose?"

"Of course I haven't!"

"But every time you do a foolish thing or get up to some mischief, I'll apply a gentle touch of the whip to the back of your legs. Do you like a gentle touch of the whip?"

"I sort of… prefer figs and apricots," mumbled Pipì, scratching his head with both hands.

"So," said Alfred, "do you accept my proposal?"

"I accept everything… except the whip, please."

"The whip is part of the deal. Otherwise, you can go away right now."

"But when you say 'gentle', it really means that you are going to strike lightly, without harming me, right?"

"I'll strike as lightly as you deserve, Pipì. So?"

"All right, then. So from now on I'll be your valet, your secretary and your travelling companion."

"Very well. Please come down."

With a jump, Pipì landed on his new master's shoulders. Alfred walked over to the table, grabbed a silver bell and rang it. The door opened and the butler walked in.

5.

"Sir?" George said.

"Please fetch the tailor from the village."

The butler gave him a blank stare.

"I want him dressed in a valet's uniform," Alfred said, pointing at Pipì with his thumb.

George raised his eyebrows, bowed and left the room. Half an hour later he came back with the tailor, a fidgety old man with a straggly beard and a pointed nose, who immediately got down to work. From a basket, he took a pair of glossy leather pumps with silk ribbons and slipped them on Pipì's feet. "Beautiful, just beautiful," the tailor whispered. Then he pushed Pipì's legs into red knee-length breeches and fastened dark-green gaiters above his ankles. "Wonderful, just wonderful," the tailor muttered, smoothing down the fabric. He wrapped a white kerchief round Pipì's neck and tied it like a cravat, then helped him into a yellow shirt and a black tailcoat. "Perfect, just perfect. Now..." He reached into his basket and produced a little top hat, complete with rosette. "There," said the tailor with a smile, placing it on Pipì's head. "You look quite the gentleman's valet now."

But Pipì didn't like his livery: the shoes were tight, the jacket uncomfortable, the cravat itchy. Surely his pink fur was much more elegant, and just as good as a uniform?

"Please bring the mirror over, George."

When the butler placed the mirror in front of him, Pipì widened his eyes in terror. Who was that hideous creature looking back at him, that abomination of nature, half monkey, half human?

He let out a squeal and turned to run away and jump out of the window, but unused to wearing shoes, he slipped and fell on his face. Still shrieking and screeching, he tried to get to his feet – but it was as if the marble floor were covered in grease, and he kept skidding and tumbling down. The humans roared with laughter.

In the end, with one desperate leap, Pipì took refuge again atop the crystal chandelier.

"Leave me," Alfred ordered the butler and the tailor, as he looked up at Pipì. "There's a good monkey," he said, gesturing to Pipì. "Come on, now, jump down."

Pipì shook his head. "Only if I can take off my shoes. I can't walk in them. I want to go barefoot."

"You'll get used to them."

"They're too painful to wear."

"After a while they won't hurt any more. Come on, come and see how beautiful you are."

Casting wary glances, Pipì climbed down the chandelier onto the table, then onto a chair, then onto the floor. He advanced towards the mirror with short, cautious steps, as if he were walking on eggshells. When he came in front of the mirror, he took one glance and flinched back.

"Oh, how ugly I am!" he cried. "Oh, Mummy, Mummy – look what they've done to your dearest little monkey! This is not Pipì... this is no longer me! They've turned me into a horrible monster! I don't want to stay here another minute... I want to go away... I want to go back home! I hate these clothes – I hate them, I hate them, I hate them!"

And as he shouted, he took off his hat and shoes and threw his cravat on the floor. In two bounds he jumped out of the window and started running across the lawn as fast as he could. But there was a whistle from the house, and he had not gone far when a firm set of teeth grabbed him by the back of his breeches and lifted him off the ground. It was Soot, the black Newfoundland.

"Let me go!" cried Pipì, flailing his arms and legs. "Let me go!"

Carrying him back to the house, Soot placed him at Alfred's feet with a satisfied bark, wagged his tail and plodded out.

"Why did you try to escape?" Alfred asked Pipì.

"Because I want to go back to Hullabaloo and live as a monkey with my mum, dad and brothers. I don't want to dress up as a human being."

"Why did you agree to be my valet, then?"

"I didn't know the job came with tight shoes and horrible clothes."

"So you really want to go?"

Pipì nodded.

"Won't you stay at least a bit longer?"

"I live far away, so I'd better be on my way."

"But aren't you tired and a little hungry?"

Pipì was, in fact, more than tired, and well beyond hungry: he swallowed, casting a wistful look at the bread and the milk on the table. "Well, maybe," he said, "since it's going to be a very long journey..."

Alfred rang the bell to call the butler.

"Sir?"

"Could you bring some fresh fruit, please?"

A few minutes later, the butler returned with a basket full of peaches, cherries, apricots, plums and pome-granates. As soon as the basket of fruit was placed on the table, Pipì jumped on a chair and began wolfing it down with both hands. Since he didn't want to appear impolite, he left the stones and some of the leaves and stalks in the basket.

When he was fit to burst, Pipì bowed and said: "I feel much better now, master Alfred. Perhaps I can go."

"Won't you take a quick look round the house with me before you leave?"

"If you wish."

Alfred led him through a series of stately rooms fitted with tapestries, rugs, precious furniture, marble busts and old paintings. They then went upstairs to the sleeping quarters. When they entered Alfred's bedroom, Pipì let out a gasp of delight: everything was so bright, tidy and lovely! And there was such a sweet smell in the air!

Alfred showed him his train sets and his most prized locomotives, his toy soldiers, his board games – which he had to play with by himself most of the time – as well as his collections of stamps and coins. He let Pipì try the wooden push-bike and the little tricycle he'd ridden when he was younger.

"This is brilliant!" Pipì shouted as he circled round the room, pedalling away. "What are those over there?"

He was pointing at two large bookshelves by the wall.

"Those?" said Alfred. "They are my books."

Pipì stopped and got off the tricycle. "How do you play with them?"

"Oh, it's easy. You just open them, read the words and look at the pictures, and they'll tell you a story. Shall I show you how it works?"

They sat in a corner of the room, and Alfred began to read aloud:

"*The Adventures of Pinocchio*, by Carlo Collodi." He turned two pages, then continued: "Once upon a time... 'There was a king!' my little readers will say – but no: they're wrong. Once upon a time, there was a piece of wood – not an expensive piece of wood: just a common log, one of those blocks that are fed to a stove or a fireplace to stoke up a fire or warm up a room."

Alfred and Pipì read for hours and hours, stopping only to eat a snack at noon and teatime, until the sky grew dark and the tale of the wooden puppet, Pinocchio, drew to its happy end.

"It was beautiful," said Pipì, when the last page was turned and the book was closed. "Will you read me another story?"

"Now?" said Alfred, smiling. "But it's really late. It will be bedtime soon, and I haven't had my supper yet. And you must be on your way before it gets too dark."

Pipì looked out of the window. Night was fast approaching: a strong wind had risen and rain was lashing down.

"Perhaps I'll keep you company during supper," he said, "and then I'll go."

"Very well."

They had dinner downstairs – Pipì stuffing himself again with peaches and plums, and only stopping when his tummy began to ache. Then the moment came when he had to leave.

"You still want to go?" asked Alfred.

Pipì nodded.

"Well, goodbye then."

Pipì shook his hand, took a deep breath and walked out of the room. When he opened the front door, he found that the night had grown darker and more menacing. There was no moon in the sky, and the wind was howling as if in anger or pain. Rain was pouring down so hard that he could hardly see the lawn. He closed the door and retraced his steps to the drawing room. On a chair he saw the bits and pieces of his uniform that he had taken off. With great difficulty, he put on the shoes and the hat, and he wrapped the kerchief round his neck, tying it in place with an absurd knot. Then he tiptoed towards the drawing room and stopped just outside. Within, Alfred was sobbing.

"He has really left," the boy was saying to himself, pressing his hands over his temples. "What shall I do now? I loved that little monkey. The Fairy brought him here. Now who will be my valet? Who will accompany me on my journey? Oh, Pipì, Pipì…"

Pipì cleared his throat. "Master Alfred, were you calling me?"

The boy sprang to his feet. "Who's there?"

"It's me."

When he saw Pipì in his livery, Alfred ran over to embrace him: it was as if he were meeting an old friend again after a very long absence.

"So you're not leaving any more?" Alfred said.

"No, Master Alfred. I'll stay with you and follow you on your long journey."

"You promise?"

"I promise."

"You swear?"

"I swear."

Alfred gave Pipì a long hug and then led him upstairs to his room, where he fell into a deep sleep after the hectic events of the past two days.

6.

A DEEP SLEEP IT MIGHT have been, but it was troubled by sinister dreams, and eventually Pipì woke up in the middle of the night with his little heart pounding in his chest. It had stopped raining, and the moon, through a crack in the clouds, cast feeble rays inside his room. A yearning crept over him: the forest, his family, his carefree life on the branches of his big leafy tree back home… Why had he agreed to stay in the service of Alfred? It was true that the fruits were delicious, and his bed so soft and comfortable, but the blank ceiling of that room was nothing like the starry blanket that covered him when he slept in the open – and anyway, weren't his dad's tales just as exciting as those told by any of Alfred's books?

Pipì got up, tiptoed to the door and looked out of his room. All was silent and dark, except for a long streak of light pouring in from a small round window at the end of the corridor. He ventured out and made a few steps towards the grand staircase, but when he spotted his own shadow moving behind him he ran back to his room, panting with fear. Dad had always warned him: shadows can chase you and whisk you away if you go around at night. But did it only happen in the forest, and not within the walls of a house? Perhaps he could wait until the moon was masked by cloud before stepping out into the night?

He plucked up his courage and, with careful steps, returned to the staircase. Just as he was about to make his way down, he froze on the spot: a glaring light – not much larger than a firefly, but brighter – was floating towards him. Once again, he rushed back to his room, but this time he tucked himself inside his bed and lay still. He heard a rhythmic creaking sound, then the door opened and George's big-nosed face, lit up by a searching candle, peered into the room for a moment before disappearing.

Pipì heaved a deep sigh. "There's nothing else for it," he said to himself. "I'll have to stay – at least until the morning."

He tried to get back to sleep, and eventually dreamed he was groping his way out of a dark forest, with the wind raging and a heavy rain forcing his eyes shut. Then the raindrops turned to hailstones – *tap*, *tap*, *tap* – and he raised his arms to protect his head, but the hailstones became boulders, and he felt crushed under their weight. When he woke up with a start, something was striking against the window panes – *tap*, *tap*, *tap*. He got up and went to look outside. On the branches of a tall tree a few yards from the walls of the house a familiar figure was waving at him. He opened the window, open-mouthed.

"Pipì! Pipì," came a whisper from the foliage.

"Dad!"

"I have finally found you! I have been looking for you for the last two days! I thought that was you earlier, on the lawn, being chased by a big black dog."

"Oh Dad, I am so happy to see you!"

"What are you wearing?"

Pipì lowered his eyes to look at his valet's uniform. The pink of his face darkened into a blush. "Oh, it's just to protect my fur," he said. "It's cold in here."

"Jump over!" said his dad.

"What, from here to there? It's a big leap."

"Come on: I've seen you jump farther than this."

"I may fall."

"I'll catch you."

"I'm not sure it's the right thing to do, Dad."

"What? Are you mad? You're living in a house dressed like a doll!"

"Because I have made a promise. To a friend, a boy, the owner of this house."

"A promise? What kind of promise?"

"I have promised to leave on a journey with him, as his manservant."

"*Man*servant? But you're a monkey! Will you abandon your family to go away on a trip with a boy? We'll all die of grief, Pipì!"

"Oh, Dad, don't say that. It was you who told me that promises must always be kept, no matter what...

Remember what happened to Ticklythroat for not keeping his?"

Pipì's dad walked to the edge of the branch, his angry frown lit up by the rays of a nearly full moon. "When are you supposed to leave?"

"I don't know," Pipì said. "Soon."

"Won't you at least say goodbye to your mum and brothers before you go?"

"Where are they?"

Pipì's dad nodded to his right. "Only a couple of hours from here. In a little wood over that hill."

"What happens if the boy, Alfred, comes to look for me while I'm away?"

"Let him look for you: you'll be back in the afternoon."

"What if his vessel leaves?"

"Let the vessel leave. Don't you think it's important to say goodbye to your family ahead of your journey?"

"I suppose…"

"Then jump!" said his dad, reaching out his hand.

Without further hesitation, Pipì climbed onto the window ledge and took a leap – one that was within his ability, but he landed on a rotten branch which gave way, plunging him into the darkness below.

There was a shriek, then a splat – and as Pipì started crying for help, Soot's furious barking erupted from a room on the ground floor. Lights came on, opening bright rectangles in the dark façade of the house.

CHAPTER 6

"Help! Help!" Pipì screeched. "I'm drowning!"

His dad scampered down the tree, and with a long stick tried to fish Pipì out of the muddy pool into which he had fallen.

"Grab at the end!" he was shouting.

"I'm going down! It's like quicksand!"

"Stay calm and hold on tight!"

The barking became even more frenzied. Voices were yelling inside the house. The front door was unlatched, and just as the light of lanterns appeared on the lawn, Pipì managed to crawl out of the pool and started running away with his dad, first through the bushes behind the house and then along the road.

When they reached the top of the hill, they turned to see if they were being chased. All they could see were two wavering lights, which seemed as distant as Soot's continuous barking.

"We're safe," said Pipì's dad.

"Only just," said Pipì, drawing his breath. "Look at me: I'm covered in mud from head to toe, and I've lost my gaiters."

"What a great loss! I'm sure your friend will give you new ones. Let's go."

They proceeded for a while along the moonlit road, then cut across a field immersed in total darkness, fumbling their way across hillocks and ditches, until they came to a dirt track, muddied by the recent rain. They hadn't walked twenty paces when a night bird flew over Pipì's head and snatched away his hat.

"Hey!" shouted Pipì. "Give that back, you thief!"

The bird squawked and disappeared.

"Oh well," said the little monkey, shrugging, "I'll have to ask Alfred to buy me another hat too."

The track led them to a tall hedge that divided two fields. There was no visible opening, so they decided to try and squeeze through it. But while Pipì was wriggling his way among the shrubs, his shirt and tailcoat got tangled up in the brambles, getting torn and shredded as a result. Only the breeches were left.

"Oh no!" gasped Pipì. "My new clothes! They're all in tatters!"

"Don't worry," said his dad. "They were all caked in mud, anyway. Your friend will buy you new ones before you leave."

"At least I've still got my cravat," Pipì said, and he brought his hand instinctively to his neck.

Now imagine his fright when, instead of his white kerchief tied around his neck, he found a tangle of nettles and foliage – and a snake slithering through them!

7.

IT WAS A VERY LARGE SNAKE, which glowed in the dark with a reddish colour, as if lit up from inside. When he reached the ground, he straightened his neck and threw a haughty stare at Pipì.

"I'm sorry," trembled the little monkey. "I didn't mean to disturb you."

The snake hissed a few words and disappeared into the grass – almost like a bright monkey tail winding its way through the field. Pipì repressed a whimper. He was glad he was still wearing his breeches to cover his bottom, so that his father couldn't see his sad little stump of a tail.

"What did he say?" said Pipì's dad.

"I don't know. I didn't catch his words." But Pipì thought he'd heard or sensed an angry warning: *The Master sent me. Your promise. He's cross.* "Perhaps I should go back to my friend, Dad," he said.

"Why?"

"Because I'm worried…"

"Worried about what?"

"Well, you've seen how many bad omens we've had. First I fell in the mud and lost my gaiters, then the night bird stole my hat, then the brambles ripped off most of my clothes, and now this snake—"

"Oh, come on, don't be a silly monkey. Can you hear those voices over there, among the trees? It's your mum and brothers: they're waiting for you. You don't want to disappoint them, do you?"

It's impossible to describe the scenes of joy and happiness at the reappearance of Pipì. His mum leapt to her feet and ran to kiss and embrace him – her youngest, whom she thought she had lost for ever. He looked so pale and gaunt in the moonlight… Where had he been? Why had he left his house in the forest? His brothers' warm greetings were soon followed by laughter and taunting.

"Where did you get *those*?" Dodò shrieked, pointing at Pipì's torn breeches.

"A couple of hours outside the forest, and he's turned all sophisticated!" said Gugù with a grimace.

Memè and Babà tried to pin him down and strip his breeches off, but Pipì wriggled himself free and pushed his brothers to the ground.

"Leave him alone," said their dad. "Can't you see he's tired? Let's have a quick bite – then all to bed."

"*Koo-ra-kah! Koo-ra-kah!*" Pipì's brothers shouted – which in monkey language means: "Dinner time!"

They laid out a humble meal of nuts and wild berries on the grass, and the young monkeys began to eat voraciously, as if they hadn't touched food for days. The nuts and the berries weren't half as tasty as Alfred's fruits, thought Pipì, but at least he was with his family now, feeling safe and comfortable.

After dinner, they each found their place around a small puddle of water that reflected the brightness of the moon, and lay down to rest. Still shaken by the recent events, and secretly guilty about breaking his promise to Alfred, Pipì struggled to fall asleep. Only when everyone around him was wheezing and snoring did his own thoughts began to wander off towards sleep – and just before his eyes closed at last, he thought he glimpsed large shadows flitting across the night sky, like giant crows with wings outstretched in flight.

"Don't move, or you're dead!" shouted a hoarse, gruff voice.

The seven monkeys woke up and raised their heads in alarm. A tall man dressed in black was holding a flaming torch that revealed an ugly bearded face crossed by an evil grin. He touched the brim of his hat and gave a rotten smile.

"Hello, monkeys," he said. "Up you get, so that my friends and I can inspect you."

Pipì gulped. They were surrounded from all sides by black-clothed men with rifles – men who were just as hideous and menacing as their leader.

"It's Ticklythroat and his gang," whispered Memè.

"The Swooping Magpies," added Babà, almost soundlessly.

"*Kree-kree-pah*," protested Pipì's dad, wanting to say: "We have nothing to give you – we're a very poor family."

"Shut up," snarled Ticklythroat. "I'll do the talking, and you'll only answer if asked."

He paced slowly round the puddle, leaning the torch forward to examine Pipì's brothers one by one. When he reached Pipì's dad, he said:

"What are you doing here in the middle of the night? Well, has your tongue tangled up all of a sudden? Where do you live?"

"*Hulla-ba-loo*," screeched Pipì's dad.

"Mmm." Ticklythroat gave this some thought. "I know the place. Lovely forest. Much safer than this wood!" He burst into gurgling laughter, followed by his companions. "Now, what do we have here?" His torch brought into full view Pipì, who was shaking like a leaf. "Oh oh: a *pink* monkey…"

"Just what you were looking for," exclaimed one of the robbers.

"Yes," rumbled Ticklythroat in a brooding tone. "*Just* what I was looking for. Come forward, little monkey."

Pipì obeyed and, looking up, felt the glare of the torch on his fur. Dad was tall, but this horrible man was a real giant.

"Who are you?" asked Ticklythroat.

"My name is Pipì."

"Ah, a talking pink monkey. You're coming with me."

"With you, sir?" gasped Pipì. "But I've just been reunited with my family! I want to go home with them."

"They'll go alone: you're coming with me."

"They won't let you take me away from them."

"Slitter, Muckrake" – Ticklythroat motioned to two of his gang – "you take care of the grown-ups. Hogwash, Scumbag, Hellhound, Crowbait – grab the little ones."

Six black figures stepped forward, grabbed the helpless monkeys under the arms and tied them to their waists.

"Please," shouted Pipì's mum in monkey language, her voice breaking, "don't kill us, don't harm our children."

"Now go," growled Ticklythroat. "Take them back to Hullabaloo. Drop them into some tall tree – not too harshly, if you please." He laughed and waved goodbye. Immediately, the six robbers lifted their arms, revealing oilskin wings shaped like those of bats. With a short run-up, they took off into the night sky, among the shrieks and cries of Pipì's family and the noise of heavy flapping.

Once they had disappeared from view, Ticklythroat gestured to the rest of his gang to move closer.

"Return to the Black Hut," he said to them, "and wait for me there. I'll be back in a few days. Tell the others."

Without waiting for their reply, he placed Pipì on his right shoulder and, torch in hand, strode out of the wood and back into the open fields.

8

WITHOUT SLACKENING his pace, Ticklythroat advanced down country roads and across rivers, meadows and groves until daybreak. As the sun rose above the horizon to wake the world, Pipì cast sideways glances at the robber's face: a frizzy black beard, bushy eyebrows, heavily lidded eyes – one of them dead and cut through by a long scar – a large nose, craggy cheekbones and pockmarked skin. Still, beneath those

grim features, Pipì thought he could see the face of the gentler Ticklythroat, the handsome young man who had lost the love of his life because of a promise unkept.

"Where are we going?" ventured Pipì after a while, scratching his nose.

Ticklythroat grunted but didn't answer.

"Are we still far away?"

Still no reply.

"How long do we have to go, Mr Assassin?"

"A thousand miles!" snarled Ticklythroat. "Why do you keep asking?"

"Because I'm starving."

"Starving? Oh, poor little monkey. Here, look in this pouch: there're all sorts of titbits inside. Careful not to eat too much!"

Pipì rummaged and rummaged in the pouch, then looked up:

"But it's empty!"

"Oh, is it?" said Ticklythroat, guffawing. "Then eat its lining or chew at the leather!"

Pipì gnawed at one of the straps, but soon gave up. "It's too tough, Mr Robber. How can you travel without food?"

"Oh, I *do* have food," Ticklythroat said with a wicked smile. "Sometimes I carry it on my shoulder."

Pipì cowered and stopped talking.

All through the morning, the afternoon and the long evening they travelled, never taking a break, and whenever they passed through a farm or a village, the shutters were quickly closed, the doors suddenly locked – the streets became deserted: Ticklythroat was infamous throughout the land.

Darkness fell before they arrived at the door of a ramshackle inn, *The Empty Larder*, standing at the outskirts of a large forest. It was close to midnight, and the cloudy sky flashed with lightning and rumbled with thunder. The door of the inn was bolted: no light could be seen inside.

"Open the door, Beanstalk!" Ticklythroat roared – Beanstalk was the innkeeper's nickname, on account of his stature and greenish complexion. "Beanstalk! You hear me? It's me, Ticklythroat! Open up!"

But Beanstalk would only open the door of his inn in the daytime. As soon as night approached, he would cautiously turn off the stove, switch off the lights, lock and bolt the door and go to bed with his little son Simon. Once he was tucked into his bed, he wouldn't open up the inn to anyone, even if he knew that the world was coming to an end outside. Should a poor traveller come knocking on his door after losing his way at night in the forest, Beanstalk, sleeping or pretending to sleep, wouldn't budge.

"Beanstalk!" Ticklythroat roared, plonking Pipì on the ground and pounding on the front door in fury. "This is my last warning! Open up or I'll come and throw you off your bed!"

When there was no reply and no sign of any light coming on inside, Ticklythroat got so angry that he began stretching his arms and legs, as if he were a shifting shadow under the rays of the sun. Extending and expanding, he became so tall that soon his neck was level with the inn's roof. Pipì watched aghast, not believing his eyes.

Once he was towering over the inn, the robber grabbed the roof with both hands and lifted it off the walls, sending pieces of thatch and stone cascading to the ground.

"Hear me now?" Ticklythroat bellowed.

Pale with terror, Beanstalk craned his head up over the blankets and looked out, recognizing in the dim light the face that was grinning at him from the sky like a horrible, dark full moon.

"Who... who is it?" he asked, pretending he had just woken up.

"Can't you see?" shouted the robber, leaning into the innkeeper's room.

"Oh," said Beanstalk, quaking, "it's you, Master Ticklythroat. What do you want from me?"

"What do I want? I want to seize you by the backside of your long johns and hurl you a hundred miles from here, that's what I want! Or kill you right here on the spot! Why didn't you open when I called?" Holding the roof up with one hand, the robber unsheathed a long dagger from his belt.

"Oh, please, Master Ticklythroat, show some mercy!"

"You deserve no mercy."

"Do it for my little Simon. If he remains here on his own, he'll be eaten by the wolves!"

"I don't want to be eaten by the wolves," exclaimed a reedy voice in a dark corner of Beanstalk's bedroom.

Ticklythroat unknitted his brows, and his face relaxed into a gentler expression. "All right," he said. "Now go and prepare some dinner."

"Of course, of course!" said Beanstalk, jumping off the bed. But his fright and confusion were such that he seemed to have forgotten how to get dressed. Thinking he was holding a sock, he kept thrusting his foot into his night cap. Abandoning the nightcap, he put on his shoes – and then, over the shoes, his socks. Slipping into his jacket – and over it his shirt and vest – he held up his trousers, apparently baffled by what they might be, and decided to fold them up and put them back in the cupboard. With a shaky hand, he lit a candle and, trying to muster a steady voice, whispered to Simon to go back to sleep.

As the giant robber lowered the roof back onto the walls of the inn, Beanstalk fumbled his way downstairs – without any trousers on – and opened the front door.

9

Ticklythroat, who had shrunk back to his normal size – which was pretty big even when he wasn't in a rage – entered the inn, shook out his wet cloak, hung up his hat on a hook and sat at the table as Beanstalk set out a plate, a glass and some cutlery. Pipì was ordered to crouch by the unlit fireplace, where a fat tabby cat was splayed out on her side, fast asleep.

"What have you got?" the robber asked Beanstalk, rubbing his belly and licking his lips at the thought of the meal to come.

"Well, I'll see what I can do," said Beanstalk, his green face greener than ever by the light of his candle. "What would you like?"

"Meat?"

"Oh, we don't have any meat, I'm afraid."

"Fish, then. Do you have fish?"

"Unfortunately we've run out of fish."

"How about cheese, then? Cheese?"

Beanstalk shook his head. "Sorry, no cheese, Master Ticklythroat."

"No meat, no fish, no cheese – what sort of inn is this?"

"Well, we're called *The Empty Larder*, not *The Midnight Feast*," the innkeeper tried to protest.

"What is it that you *have*, then?" growled the robber.

"Plenty of stale bread, and some tomatoes to make it softer, as well as salt, pepper and olive oil to make it tastier. Oh, and we also have some fresh fruits."

Pipì's ears pricked up.

Ticklythroat banged his fist on the table. "Bring me everything you've got," he said. "And two bottles of wine."

Beanstalk came back with the food, and the robber began to eat and drink with great appetite. From time to time he glanced at Pipì, who observed his munching with wistful eyes and a slavering mouth.

"Still hungry?" Ticklythroat shouted, once he'd eaten all the bread and drunk an entire bottle of wine, wiping his lips with the back of his hand. The little monkey nodded hopefully. "Then why don't you come and join me for the dessert? Beanstalk, grab another plate for my friend here."

Pipì took his place opposite the robber as the inn-keeper set out a plate and a napkin in front of him and left the candle in the middle of the table.

"It's very kind of you, Your Assassinship," said Pipì. "I knew that under that harsh exterior was hidden a gentle heart."

Ticklythroat shifted in his chair. He brought the fruit basket close to his chest and frowned at Pipì with a piercing look.

"What do you mean, 'harsh exterior'?" he said. "Do you think I'm ugly?"

"Ugly?" gasped Pipì. "No, not at all! I have met many humans in my life, but I've never seen the likes of you. You're very handsome – in fact, you're the handsomest man I've ever seen!"

"You should have seen me years go," said the robber in a low grumble, filling another glass of wine, "when I was young. Then I really was handsome. Tell him, Beanstalk, wasn't I handsome then, eh?"

"Oh yes," nodded the innkeeper with a taut expression, sensing trouble. "Handsome, very handsome! Bright and shining like the sun!"

"Like the sun at noon!" Pipì chipped in, glancing at the basket of fruits in expectation.

Ticklythroat downed his glass and turned an even fiercer stare on Pipì. "Are you saying I'm like the sunset now? Fading? Going down? Becoming nothing?"

"You're like a *wonderful* sunset, Mr Assassin," said Pipì, scrambling to correct himself, "a sunset more glorious and resplendent than any sunrise has ever been! A sunset to last for eternity!"

"I see." The robber became thoughtful and sullen-looking, and ate all the cherries and the apricots in the basket, spitting out the stones onto his plate one by one, as Pipì looked on. He downed another glass of wine and pushed the basket towards the middle of the table.

"Would *you* like some fruit too?" he asked.

The little monkey nodded.

"Then let me serve you myself." Ticklythroat stood up, and with his fat fingers picked imaginary fruits from the basket and deposited them onto Pipì's empty plate. He sat down again and turned his gaze on the little monkey's famished face, studying its puzzled expression and shifting eyes, which kept darting between the basket and the plate.

"What is it?" the robber said. "Not hungry any more? Eat."

Sighing at the cruel joke, Pipì brought the invisible fruits to his mouth and began munching them as if they were real.

"Good, aren't they?" Ticklythroat taunted him.

"Mmm. Exquisite."

"Have some more, have some more. You won't get indigestion from this lot."

"OK, thank you."

The robber was in no rush to bring the pantomime to an end, and only when the candle flame began to flicker, after he had downed the last mouthful of wine from his second bottle, did he stand up and yawn.

"Enough now. Time to go to bed. I think I'm going to lie on this bench. You, you greedy little monkey" – pointing at Pipì – "return to your corner, and don't move from there." Then he turned to the innkeeper, Beanstalk, who was himself half asleep. "And you make sure you wake me up at the break of dawn. Not a minute later."

"Of course," said Beanstalk. "Don't worry: you can have a peaceful sleep."

The innkeeper, his bare knees knocking against each other, took the candle and went back to his bedroom, plunging them into darkness.

10.

PIPÌ'S BRIGHT, WIDE-OPEN EYES twinkled in the dark. Ticklythroat's growling snore was echoed by a wheezing sound from upstairs and accompanied by the tabby cat's deep purr, not to mention the *drip-drip-drip* of the tap in the kitchen sink: roar-hiss-purr-*drip-drip-drip*, roar-hiss-purr-*drip-drip-drip*. Sleeping that night was out of the question.

When, hours later, the moon emerged from the clouds to cast a pale ray through the windows of the inn, Pipì tiptoed around the room to see if he could find a way to escape. The heavy wooden front door was locked, and its creaking would have woken up a sleeping buffalo. The door to the upstairs rooms had been locked by the prudent Beanstalk. The windows were bolted shut, but they were big enough for him to get out if he could just find a way to break them without making too much noise – or, maybe, by making a lot of noise…

In a corner of the room he found Ticklythroat's boots. Hmmm… and on the table there was olive oil, salt, pepper…

He grabbed the jar of olive oil and poured the greasy substance all over the floor, in front of the bench where the robber was sound asleep. After that, he sprinkled a good dose of salt and pepper on the fellow's fat fingers. Then he undid the laces of Ticklythroat's boots. Taking one of the laces, he tied one end to Ticklythroat's belt and the other end to the cat's tail. He stepped back to examine his handiwork – a very good job, he told himself.

Now he was ready. This was the time. Jumping lightly onto the table, he hurled one of the empty wine bottles at the window with all his strength.

Crash! Ticklythroat, half drunk, jolted his head up and instinctively rubbed his sleepy eyes. The sting of salt and pepper made him yowl and jump off his bench to his feet – but as he did so, he slipped on the greasy floor and fell down, dragging towards him the poor cat, who landed on his beard and began to scratch away in fright for all she was worth.

"Aah!" the robber howled, trying to wrench the cat off his face. "I'm blinded, I'm blinded!"

Among the shouting and squealing and mayhem, Pipì sneaked out through the broken window and darted away through the dimly lit forest. He had only gone fifty yards when he heard the inn door being unlatched and the roar of Ticklythroat's raging voice:

"I'll get you yet, little monkey! You hear me? And when I do, I'll make a nice hat out of your fur!"

Without looking back, Pipì fled as fast as he could through the trees and tall bushes, terrified that the furious Ticklythroat might stretch his limbs and catch up with him in a few long strides. But the robber wasn't his only fear: the shadows of the forests might steal him away. And what was that noise? A pack of wolves? Or some other hungry, ferocious beast of the wild? Panting, thrashing through the undergrowth, he pressed on in no particular direction.

It was only later in the morning, when the light of noon pierced the foliage above, warming the grassy ground, that Pipì stopped to have a rest by the edge of a brook, which wound its way among the trees. He took off his tattered breeches, dipped them in the water and used them to wipe his face. As he drank from his cupped hands, he noticed, among the pebbles on the bed, a scatter of plum and peach stones. There must be fruit trees nearby.

As he walked away from the stream, he heard voices – monkey voices, shrieks, shouts – perhaps a big family party, like the rumbustious celebrations that were common in his own forest? Or something more dangerous? He advanced cautiously, until the noise grew to a deafening din.

In a clearing of the forest, hundreds of monkeys were engaged in violent combat. There appeared to be two factions: the black monkeys, who were wearing coconut-shell helmets and brandishing long sticks, and the brown monkeys, who used wicker shields and headgear for protection, and supple whips to lash their opponents. The Blacks' rearguard showered the enemy

with a barrage of conkers, which was answered by volley after volley of rotten fruit from the Browns. In the middle of the field, a disorderly monkey-to-monkey scuffle was raging, in which no blow was spared. Among the punching, kicking, scratching, shouting and biting of the two armies rose the warring figures of the two generals, one wearing a palm headdress, the other a donkey's skull as marks of their authority. It was the latter, the general of the Blacks, who suddenly lifted his staff and shouted above the clamour of the battle:

"*Tatà-ruk Pipì!*"

At a stroke, everyone stopped fighting. The monkeys who were flailing on the ground got to their feet; those who were wrestling in close combat disentangled themselves; the volleys of conkers and rotten fruit ceased on both sides; staves, whips and shields were laid down; and all eyes turned to look at the little pink monkey

– who, not quite knowing what he was doing or why he was doing it, stepped out of the shadows and came into full view in the clearing.

The two generals nodded to each other and, as their soldiers parted and made way for them, walked with regal swagger towards Pipì. They stopped in front of him and exchanged a few mumbled words, then uncovered their heads and bowed down low, their heads touching the ground that only moments ago had been a battlefield.

"*Tatà-ruk Pipì!*" repeated the general of the Browns, with his forehead still on the ground. "The pink monkey has arrived!"

"Long live our new emperor!" said the general of the Blacks.

11.

J UBILATION! Helmets flew through the air, and
shouts of "Long live Pipì! Long live the emperor!"
resounded through the forest. Pipì looked on in amaze-
ment, not sure what to say or do. At length, he raised
his hand to speak, and the monkeys fell silent.

"Thank you, my kind subjects," he said in an uncer-
tain tone. "I'll prove to you that I am worthy of your
trust."

Great cries of joy and happiness started up again, as
the soldiers who only a few minutes earlier were locked
in combat now danced together and embraced. Pipì
looked down at the two generals and invited them to
get to their feet.

"Why did you choose me to be your emperor?" he
asked.

The generals exchanged a knowing look. "He wants
to test our knowledge of our faith," said the Brown
chief to the Black, nudging his elbow.

"As our elders say in their sacred wisdom," the
Black general announced with a solemn voice, "a Pink
Monkey will come to reign over the Browns and the
Blacks. All their wars will end, and the emperor's word
will put an end to all their disagreements."

"*Tatà-ruk Pipì!*" cried the Brown commander.

"*Tatà-ruk Pipì! Tatà-ruk Pipì!*" shouted all the others in exultation.

"To the emperor's temple!"

"To the emperor's temple! To the emperor's temple!"

Six monkeys, three brown and three black, trotted up towards Pipì, bearing a rudimentary straw-built throne between them. The litter chair was eased onto the ground, and the new emperor was invited to climb onto it.

"I'm not quite used to this," Pipì said, demurring. "If it's all the same to you, I'd rather scamper about on my own four feet as usual."

The two generals looked at each other, their foreheads crinkling up into identical frowns.

"But that's not possible, Your Highness!" said the Black chief.

"Why?" asked Pipì.

"Because an emperor who goes on foot is no longer an emperor – merely a common monkey!"

"But I could give *orders* to be allowed to go on foot…"

"Indeed you could, Your Pinkship. But it is an emperor's privilege to do everything according to established rules, not according to his own whim."

"I see," said Pipì, scratching his nose. "Very well, let's go." He jumped onto the throne and signalled to the bearers to carry him.

The litter weaved its way through the armies, which gathered behind to form a long stream of soldiers, at the head of which marched the two generals. They soon reached the Temple, a wooden mansion that had previously been inhabited by humans for hundreds of moons. The whole monkey population of the forest assembled to witness the coronation of Pipì, the emperor.

At the sound of horns and drums, the elders of the two tribes presented Pipì with the crown – a ring of dates on a wicker frame, set with ruby-like little cherries – and the sceptre, made out of carved sugar. As the crown was raised up and placed on Pipì's head, and as the sceptre was handed to him, the crowd burst into rapturous cheers and applause. Pipì nodded modestly, and just stopped himself from nibbling on one of the dates of his crown and taking a lick at his sceptre.

He was paraded into the Temple, where a long table had been laid out for a banquet, and seated in the middle, surrounded by all the elders of the Browns and the Blacks. *I am hungrier than Snapper!* he thought, smelling all the food that was waiting in the wings. Before the celebratory lunch began, each elder gave a long speech in honour of the new emperor – two hours passed, and the little pink money stifled yawn after yawn. When, at last, the first dishes were served, Pipì's eyes rolled and his tongue lolled – the elders were getting platefuls of every sort of fresh fruit, whereas his plate was either ignored or granted one or two shrivelled wild berries. Course followed course, and while his stomach remained almost empty, the elders kept munching away and drinking milk and honey in good cheer, gorging themselves, getting fat. Pipì waved one of the waiters over.

"Why are you ignoring me when you're serving the fruit?" he whispered in his ear.

The waiter smiled – such a wise new emperor they had, always looking to test the wisdom of his subjects! "We know that emperors have no interest in food, Your Highness," replied the waiter. "We know that they affect a certain disdain for such earthly things, to demonstrate their superiority. You are doing extremely well, Your Highness. Would you like some water?"

"Yes."

"Maybe half a glass," said the waiter.

The banquet didn't come to an end until the sun had already set. The elders withdrew to their trees, bloated and burping, while the emperor was escorted to his bedroom by his loyal generals. As he climbed the stairs, Pipì's only hope was that he could sleep his hunger off.

He was led to a large, empty room, in the middle of which lay a heap of rough brushwood. Pipì took off his crown and scratched his head.

"I don't understand," he said. "What is this?"

"This is your royal chamber, Your Highness," said the Black chief. "The bramble bed."

"The bramble bed? A bed made of brambles?" gasped Pipì. "And why don't I sleep on the branch of a tree, like every other monkey in the forest?"

"Such wisdom in his questions!" the Brown commander mumbled to the Black commander, who nodded in admiration. "Your Highness," explained the Brown commander, "this bed is devised so that you can always be on the alert. You see, with great authority comes great responsibility."

"And what are those?" Pipì asked, pointing at a stack of round white things lined against the wall.

"As you know, Your Highness, these are the skulls of our past, mighty, revered emperors," said the Brown general, "who were either killed in battle or executed at the end of their term, as is our custom. They'll watch over your sleep and ward off any evil spirit."

The new emperor looked at him. Executed? At the end of their term? Pipì swallowed. How long was a term?

"There is some fresh water for you in that bowl, Your Highness," said the Black general. "Although, in your wisdom, I understand you won't drink much. If you need anything during the night, please ask the guards outside your room."

The generals bowed their heads and departed, taking all light with them, leaving Pipì in almost complete darkness.

12.

"**I**'M NOT SURE I LIKE being the emperor," Pipì was thinking as he lay on the floor, as far away as possible from the menacing, vacant stares of the skulls. "Food is scant, sleep is prickly – and as a final reward you get butchered in battle or your head chopped off on the executioner's block!"

He yawned and tried to close his eyes, but the emperors of the past seemed to be whispering stories to him – stories of violence and terror, which made it difficult for him to fall asleep. In the end, after twisting and turning on the hard wooden floor for an hour, he dozed off – only to bolt upright suddenly.

"Long live the emperor! Long live Pipì!" came the cheers outside, accompanied by loud music.

"Come out on the balcony to greet us!"

"We love you!"

One of the elders, the master of ceremonies, entered the room with a torch.

"Your Highness! Your Highness!" he shouted, shining his light around the room until he found Pipì. "Your subjects are celebrating your arrival. They want to see you: get up and go to the balcony!"

Pipì grumbled a few sleepy bad words, then staggered out onto the balcony, yawning. Below, at the sight of their ruler, the crowd went wild, and the sound of horns and riotous shrieking redoubled in the night air.

"Long live the emperor! Long live Pipì!" came the chant from both the brown and the black monkeys.

"Your Highness," whispered the master of ceremonies in Pipì's ear, "speak to your subjects. Grant them your wisdom! Say something profound!"

Pipì raised his hand and gave a pale smile, and the crowd fell silent.

"Thank you, my dear friends," he said, "or rather, my dear subjects. Your music is wonderful, and you have excellent voices. I'm overjoyed. And I'm very happy for you too." He scratched his cheek, then added: "Er, I think that's just about all I've got for the moment, so I'll say goodnight, and, er, yeah – see you tomorrow."

There was rowdy cheering, and the crowd dispersed. Pipì returned inside and the master of ceremonies bowed his head and left the room. Two more sleepless hours followed, until just at the point he was about to doze off, the clamorous chanting kicked off again.

"We want to see the emperor! We want to see the emperor!"

With drowsy eyes, he stumbled out onto the balcony. A large group of brown monkeys had gathered below, with banners held high and military whips in their hands. They welcomed Pipì's appearance with shouts of joy and wild whooping.

Pipì raised his hand to ask for silence. "My dear brown-furred subjects," he said, suppressing a yawn behind his hand, "what can I do for you at this time of night?"

"We want the sun!" said one of the elders of the Browns. "The nights are too long and cold for us. We want the sun, or there will be war!"

"We want the sun! We want the sun!" echoed the crowd of brown monkeys.

Pipì raised his hand. "I cannot give you the sun right now, but I guarantee you that the sun will rise tomorrow morning! And as a token of my promise, you can see its image above my head." He pointed at the window pane behind him, where the bright face of the moon was reflected.

"Hurrah!" cheered the monkeys. "We'll have our sun tomorrow! Long live the emperor! Hurrah for the emperor!"

The brown monkeys left, and Pipì returned to his warm spot on the floor and waited for sleep. But despite his exhaustion, his eyes remained wide open – surely some elder would shake him awake, even if he were to nod off. But after three more hours of twisting and turning, as the sun peeked over the line of the horizon, at last he was in the land of sleep – then Pipì jolted up at the sound of drums and yelling outside.

"We want to see the emperor! We want to see the emperor!"

A crowd of black monkeys, holding their banners and brandishing their staves, had assembled under the Temple's balcony. Pipì, dragging himself outside, raised his hand, and a few moments later there was silence.

"What can I do for you?" said the pink monkey. "Does no one ever sleep in this forest?"

"Your Highness," said one of the Blacks' elders, "we have heard that you have promised our old enemies, the Browns, that the sun will shine over the coming day. We've come here to protest and demand rain instead. Too much sun will make the fruit less juicy, and we black monkeys cannot stand the heat. So give us rain, or there will be war!"

"Give us rain! Give us rain!" chanted all the Blacks in unison.

Pipì raised his hand again. "I cannot give you rain right now, but—"

"No, we want rain! We want rain now!" shouted the crowd.

"—but I promise you that rain will come soon. Now close your eyes, and I'll give you a token of my pledge to you." He took the bowl from inside and showered its contents on the black monkeys, who opened their eyes and yelled:

"Rain, rain! The emperor is giving us rain! Long live the emperor! Hurrah for the emperor!"

When the Browns heard that the Blacks had been promised rain, they gathered underneath the balcony and started to protest. The Blacks arrived too, and scuffles ensued between the two tribes, until their generals restored some order and agreed that this matter of sun or rain was to be decided by the emperor: as the elders maintained in their sacred wisdom, the emperor was the only being who could put an end to all disagreements.

Both factions called out, asking for Pipì to come and speak to them, but the balcony window remained closed, even though behind the windows could be glimpsed the vague silhouette of the crowned emperor, sitting regally and still. The monkeys banged on their drums, blew their horns and yelled and hollered. Conkers and rotten fruit began raining down on the balcony, but the emperor himself still remained unmoved behind the window.

In the end, the two generals and a small group of soldiers from both sides entered the Temple, ran upstairs and, after dismissing the guards, stormed into the emperor's room. In front of the balcony window was a heap of brambles crudely put together in the shape of a monkey, surmounted by a skull with the emperor's crown – though all the cherry-studded dates had been eaten. Above, the skylight was ajar.

Reinforcements of soldiers were called in, and every room of the Temple, every nook and cranny – from the roof through to the basement – was inspected. But the emperor had escaped.

13.

THE BROWNS AND THE BLACKS poured out into the forest in all directions, beating the bushes and shrieking in fury as they searched for Pipì. Not far ahead of them, the little monkey was plunging through the thick woods, trying to get as much advantage as possible over his pursuers. Being unfamiliar with the surroundings, however, he gulped in terror – maybe he was just running around in circles, about to be captured at any moment? When he fell down into the remnants of an old campfire, he rolled himself in the ash: if he couldn't turn himself into a brown- or black-furred monkey, he could at least make himself a grey one rather than a pink one. Otherwise it might not be long before another skull was added to the collection of mighty and revered dead emperors in the bramble-bed room.

After wandering through the forest for hours and hours, he came to the clearing where the two warring tribes had welcomed him as their emperor only yesterday and cautiously looked through a gap in a big bush. There, under the fierce sun of noon, he found the Browns and the Blacks engaged in a new battle, among shrieks, shouts, kicks, bites, punches and volleys of conkers and rotten fruit.

"Sun!" shouted the general of the Browns, his face disfigured by anger, as he lashed the Blacks' commander with his whip.

"Rain!" yelled the other, landing a blow on his opponent's head with his staff. "We want rain!"

Pipì gave an involuntary smile and, retreating among the bushes, scampered away.

As the sun descended in the west and a shower of rain washed the ash from his fur, Pipì emerged from the forest into an open plain at the top of a hill. He looked around: the landscape seemed strangely familiar. There was a little road winding its way downhill, and there were rolling fields in the distance. And look – the ivy-covered façade of the large country house in the valley below – and how could he forget that raucous bark resounding through the air?

"Alfred's house!" he shouted in delight. "And if Soot is still there, his master must be there too! Perhaps, if I explain what happened, he'll forgive me and take me with him on his journey! Then I can keep my promise!"

Tired and famished though he was, he started down the road to Alfred's house with a new spring in his step, and had almost reached the front lawn when he saw six black figures hovering high up in the darkening sky.

CHAPTER 13

There was a series of strident whistles, and before he had time to flee, he was surrounded by Ticklythroat and the Swooping Magpies. With two long strides, the leader of the gang reached Pipì and lifted him up by the scruff of his neck.

"Did you really think you could escape from me, little monkey?" the robber bellowed. "I told you I would get you yet!"

"Don't hurt me, Mr Assassin," pleaded Pipì, trembling.

"Hurt you? No, I won't *hurt* you: I'll just make one big mouthful of you!" He roared with laughter, then gestured to his companions: "Go back to the hut now. I'll see you all when I've finished my business with this little sneak here."

The robbers took off and flapped away, disappearing over the edge of the hill. Ticklythroat placed Pipì on the ground and levelled a hard stare at him.

"Don't you dare escape again, you hear?" he growled. "If you so much as take half a step away from me, you're a dead monkey. You understand?" Pipì nodded, his face rigid. "We don't have far to go. In fact, we've already arrived."

"Arrived?" said Pipì. "But this is where Master Alfred lives."

"I know," said Ticklythroat, "and this is where I was taking you all along – you silly monkey."

"I… I don't understand," said Pipì with a shaky voice. "Why would you want to take me back to Master Alfred?"

"Because the lady is angry."

"Which lady?"

"Bella, the Fairy with Turquoise Hair. She came to me in a dream the other night: she asked me to go and find you, and take you back to the boy, her fairy godchild. She said you had promised to accompany him on his journey: and she's *not* someone to take broken promises too lightly." Here Ticklythroat's face darkened.

"Oh, Mr Robber," Pipì exclaimed, hugging Ticklythroat around the neck, "you should have told me you wanted to take me here! I'll be so happy to see Master Alfred again! And I'm sure he'll be delighted too!"

"And I can finally keep a promise to Bella," Ticklythroat mumbled to himself, frowning. "Now, jump on my shoulder and follow me."

Pipì readily obeyed, and the robber advanced onto the lawn with long steps towards the entrance of the house.

14.

NO SOONER HAD THE ROBBER knocked on the door than the sound of furious barking could be heard inside.

"Keep quiet, Soot!" came George's voice. "Now, be a good dog. Go in there and be quiet!"

The barking stopped, and the door opened slightly to reveal the butler's big nose. Still afraid of the dog, Pipì hid behind Ticklythroat's leg.

"Oh, you're already here?" George said, giving the scruffy, unkempt man the once-over. "We were expecting you in an hour or two. Anyway, the luggage is ready in the hall. You can start loading it onto the coach."

"I'm not the coachdriver," was Ticklythroat's gruff reply, "and I'm not here to haul your luggage around. I'm here to talk to the boy. Is he in?"

George studied the man's appearance again, and fixed his stare on his dead eye. "It depends," he said.

"Well, tell him I brought his pet back, will you?" Ticklythroat reached behind his leg and lifted Pipì into view.

The butler widened his eyes and raised his brows. "Oh, the pink monkey. You've brought it back, have you? I'll see if he can speak to you."

"Why can't I just come in?"

George glanced at the robber's muddy boots. "Please wait here. I won't be long."

A few moments later, a cry of joy could be heard from one of the rooms within. Alfred emerged at the other end of the entrance hall and, seeing Pipì, ran towards him with open arms.

"Oh, Pipì, Pipì!" he exclaimed, embracing his friend. "I thought I'd lost you for ever! Where did you go? I looked for you everywhere! I was just about to leave, and I was so sorry to have to go on my own! Will you come with me now?"

"Of course, Master Alfred," Pipì said, with tears welling in his eyes. "I'll come with you and accompany you on your journey – I promised I would."

Only then did Alfred notice the big, bearded, scary-looking man standing by the doorway. He went over to him and gave him a friendly handshake.

CHAPTER 14

"Thank you so much, sir, for bringing back Pipì," Alfred said. "You don't know how grateful I am to you. What can I do to compensate you for your trouble?"

"Perhaps," intervened George, reappearing behind the boy, "we could give the gentleman some money?"

Ticklythroat shook his head. "I don't want any money," he said. "This is something I had to do. For a friend. A mutual friend." He scratched his cheek and heaved a deep sigh. "Well, I must be going now. You take care, young lad, and keep an eye on little pink-face here: he's a crafty one, you know?"

They watched Ticklythroat as he lumbered down the lawn with long, heavy strides. When he reached the foot of the hill, he turned for a moment, raising his arm to wave goodbye. They waved back, just before his figure disappeared in the dusk of the evening. Was it just his imagination, Pipì wondered, or was the man who smiled at them from the distance no longer the scarred, ugly robber who had been terrorizing the land for years and years, but the gentle, handsome youth who had been in love with Bella?

"The coach will be here in about an hour," Alfred told Pipì, "and the ship is sailing at midnight. There're still a few things to pack for the journey, but you'll have time for dinner and a good wash. George, please ask the tailor in immediately: we need a new uniform for Pipì. Oh, but what's that?"

Pipì followed Alfred's gaze and turned his head to look down his back. There, in all its pink, swivelling fluffiness, his tail had sprouted back to life.

"Oh, my tail!" Pipì shouted, as he stroked and embraced it. "My lovely tail! The turquoise rabbit was right: she told me I would get it back if I fulfilled my promise! Now I can face my family without shame. Do you think we could pass by the forest of Hullabaloo on the way to our ship? I would love to say goodbye to Mum and Dad and my brothers before we leave."

"Of course," said Alfred. "But first let's go and have something to eat. I can't wait to hear what you did over the last three days."

"Oh, Master Alfred," Pipì said. "If I begin to tell you what happened to me, you'll never believe it!"

EXTRA MATERIAL
FOR YOUNG READERS

THE WRITER

Carlo Collodi was born in Florence on 24th November 1826. His real name was Carlo Lorenzini: he took the pen name by which he is famous today from the small town between Lucca and Pistoia in Tuscany where his mother was born and where he spent part of his childhood. Carlo's parents, Domenico and Angiolina, worked in the household of a nobleman, Marquess Ginori: his father was a cook, his mother a housemaid.

Carlo was the first-born, and he had nine siblings. Five of them died in their infancy, and he was himself a sickly child when young. Although his family lived in reduced circumstances, he was able to get a good education thanks to the help of the Ginori family. He initially trained to become a priest, but in 1842 moved on to study rhetoric and philosophy at a religious school in Florence.

In 1844, having completed his studies, Carlo started working at the Florentine bookshop Piatti, which also had a small press. It was there, as he penned reviews for the bookshop's catalogue, that his writing career began.

At the outbreak of the First Italian War of Independence in 1848, Carlo joined the Tuscan army as a volunteer and fought the Habsburg troops at the Battle of Curtatone and Montanara. When he returned to Florence, he started a prolific career as a journalist, critic, translator, humorist and author, writing on many subjects ranging from theatre and music to literature. It was in 1856 that he first used his pseudonym "Collodi".

After another short experience in the army during the 1859 Second Italian War of Independence, Carlo became a theatre censor, reviewing works to be approved for the stage – and a few years later, at the invitation of the Ministry of Education, he was asked to join a panel of experts working on a dictionary of spoken Italian.

It was only in 1875, in his advanced middle age, that Carlo turned to children's literature. The publisher Paggi asked him to translate some of the most famous stories by Charles Perrault, Jeanne-Marie Leprince de Beaumont and Marie-Catherine d'Aulnoy (including 'Little Red Riding Hood', 'Sleeping Beauty', 'Puss in Boots' and 'Cinderella'), which he collected the following year in a volume entitled *Fairy Tales*. He then began a series of educational books for Italian schools, featuring a naughty boy called Giannettino as the hero.

The success of this series prompted Carlo to write more books for children. In July 1881, in the first issue of the *Giornale per i bambini* (*The Children's Magazine*), he published the initial instalment of *The Story of a Marionette*, which was later to become *The Adventures of Pinocchio*. The writing of this book, however, was far from easy: when he was a third of the way through, Carlo left the puppet hanging by the neck from a tree, perhaps intending to bring the tale to a sad and abrupt end. It was only after two long breaks and much pleading from the magazine that he was able to complete the story in 1883.

Carlo had become a successful writer now, but he regarded his children's tales as inferior to his more serious work, and it was with reluctance that he embarked on another story for the *Giornale per i bambini* – of which by now he had become the director – *The Adventures of Pipì the Pink Monkey*.

Again, work was very slow, and Carlo lost faith and interest in the project more than once. A few chapters appeared in the *Giornale per i bambini* in August 1883, but they were followed by a long break. Throughout 1884, the young readers of the magazine wrote to the author asking for more instalments of *Pipì*, but they had to wait until the end of the following year to see the story completed.

Now at the height of his success, Carlo was celebrated as the leading living Italian children's author. He did not live long, however, to enjoy his fame: as he came back home on 26th October 1890, he collapsed on the doorstep of his house and died. He never lived to know that his main creation, Pinocchio – only reprinted once in book form during his lifetime – would one day become one of the most popular characters in children's literature and give him worldwide renown.

THE BOOK

The Adventures of Pipì was written immediately after *Pinocchio*, and it shares many features with its more famous counterpart. Most evident are the similarities between their two main characters, the pink monkey and the wooden puppet: both of them show a penchant for lying, disobedience and general naughtiness. Also similar is the madcap nature of their adventures, and the way they both overcome life-threatening situations, coming out unscathed (more or less) in the end.

The two stories contain some of the same characters too. One is the Fairy with Turquoise Hair, which in *Pipì* is mentioned a few times, but only reveals herself in disguise as the rabbit with turquoise fur. The other character is even more difficult to spot: it is Pinocchio himself, appearing in *Pipì* as the ten-year-old boy Master Alfred. There is no mention of this in the story itself, but in the 8th January 1885 issue of the *Giornale per i bambini* Collodi, apologizing for his constant delays and broken promises to continue *The Adventures of Pipì*, published the following 'Explanation to the Young Readers of the *Giornalino*':

Florence, 3rd [January] 1885

My dear young Friends,

I know full well that you have complained about me – I have even received a letter from Rome about it!

The reason of your complaint? That I haven't kept my promise to continue the story of Pipì the Pink Monkey.

And you're quite right. So learn from me: when you promise something, you must keep your promise, unless you want to make a fool of yourself in the eyes of all the people who know you and think highly of you.

In fact, talking of unkept promises, I'd like to ask you a favour. If, during the recent Christmas and New Year holidays, you happened to promise that you'd be studying harder and more diligently, please *remember to honour your word. Otherwise you know what's going to happen, don't you? Your mums and dads, seeing their hopes dashed, will say in a mocking, reproachful tone: "You're such good boys and girls!... After all your promises, you've done just like Collodi: he promises and promises and then... see you later!"*

So you will understand that, although I never promised more studying, I'd be taking my own share of flak from these reproaches addressed to you, poor devil that I am!

As to the rest, now that I've confessed my sin, please allow me to give you a very short explanation in my defence.

Well then, this is how things are.

One fine morning last year, I was about to pick up my pen again and continue the story I had left midway through, when I heard the doorbell ring.

"Who is it?" I asked.

"Someone who's looking for you."

"And what would that someone look like?"

"Well, at first glance one might take him for a little monkey."

"Then tell him I am not at home and I won't see any little monkeys."

Just as I said this, the door to my room was suddenly thrown open wide, and a shrill, screeching, insolent voice – like that of a fussing puppy dog – shouted at a high pitch:

"I hope at least you'll be seeing me."

"And who would you be?" I asked the little fellow in front of me, smartly dressed in a travelling suit.

"Who would I be? So you don't recognize me?"

"No."

"Look at me carefully."

"I have."

"You still don't recognize me?"

"No, I don't."

"I am…"

"Come on, tell me: who are you?"

"I am Pipììììììì!…"

"How could it be? You're Pipì? The pink monkey?"

"The very one, in person."

"I should have guessed it. Please, sir, take a seat," said I, offering him a chair that was covered in satin with large red-and-yellow floral patterns.

Without waiting to be asked twice, with the aplomb of an English diplomat, Pipì took a majestic jump and perched atop the back of the chair.

"To what do I owe the pleasure of seeing you here in Florence? Where are you travelling from?"

"I've come from San Francisco in California. I was in that city a few months ago, and I chanced to see this Giornalino you're running. And, as I was leafing through it, I found the story of my life and my adventures. Let me tell you this, Signor Collodi: that story is pure libel – what a beautiful present you gave me!"

"Why?"

"And you're asking me 'why'? How could you – for example – tell every child in Italy that I lost my tail – and that it was gobbled up by an old croc?"

"But I was assured it was true…"

"True or not – what would you say if tomorrow every newspaper announced that your pet cat had eaten your tail?"

"Oh please, don't even joke about it! It would break my heart!"

"Well then, can I ask you a favour, to make up for the hurt you caused me?"

"Sure, tell me."

"Please promise me not to continue your story until I have given you some notes written by my good self in my own noble hand."

"This I can promise you. But when will I get these notes?"

"When I come back from my trip."

"Talking of trips – could you tell me who is this boy who is travelling with you?"

"It's anyone's guess. I know that his name is Alfred and that his mum, when she writes to him, always signs herself 'Your loving Fairy with Turquoise Hair'."

"But this boy, Alfred, when he was younger – where did he live? What did he do?"

"He told me himself that when he was younger he was a wooden puppet. Then he turned into a lovely little boy, very clever and kind-hearted – like few others these days! Would you like to see his portrait? Here it is."

And at these words Pipì gave me Alfred's portrait, as well as his, which I thought very lifelike and expressive.

Then, as he was about to leave, he shook my hand and said:

"See you in a few months."

Many months have gone by since then, but Pipì hasn't come back. It was only the other day, on New Year's Eve, that I found on my table the pink monkey's notes. *And with the help of these notes, my dear young friends, I promise you I will be able to pick up again the long-abandoned story. And I also promise you, when I give you the new chapters, to show you the* portraits *of Alfred and his friend Pipì.*

C. Collodi

As we have seen, Collodi intentionally inserted some cross-references from *Pinocchio* into the tale of the little pink monkey. *Pipì,* then, can be seen as a kind of ironic retelling of the wooden puppet's story. In it, we are again presented with a non-human hero with many rascally traits that goes through scrapes and dangers before finding his real self. But whereas in *Pinocchio* the puppet is eventually transformed into a flesh-and-blood boy, Pipì's experiences outside the forest convince him that he very much wants to remain a little monkey.

CHARACTERS

Pipì
Pipì is a little monkey from the forest of Hullabaloo. He is different from all his brothers and the other monkeys in the forest, because his fur is "coloured like a rose". That is not the only thing that sets him apart: he is more like a mischievous young boy than a monkey, and his greatest passion is to copy humans and everything they do. This streak in his character and his natural

love of fun and adventure prompt him to explore the world around him and land him in all sorts of trouble. From his bitter experiences outside the forest he will learn that he must follow the advice of his elders and, above all, tell the truth and keep his promises.

Alfred
Alfred is a ten-year-old boy who lives in a country house with his butler George and his dog Soot. His world is very orderly and organized: his room is tidy and his meals are served at specific times. He is planning to visit his parents overseas and is scheduled to leave on a boat soon. When a sack is brought to his door and its contents revealed, he knows this is the present his fairy godmother had promised him: a pet pink monkey that will accompany him on his voyage. Alfred – himself a wooden puppet who has become a boy – shows Pipì what could happen to him if he behaves well and stops being naughty, telling fibs and breaking his promises. Pipì, however, has other ideas in mind, and is unwilling to wear human clothes and adopt human ways.

Ticklythroat
Ticklythroat is a gruff, bearded robber who, together with his gang of thieves, terrorizes the land outside the forest of Hullabaloo. Legend has it that he was as handsome once as he is now scarred and ugly: a broken promise is what cost him his fiancée Bella and his good

looks. But bringing Pipì back and making him keep his own word to Alfred may give Ticklythroat a final chance to prove himself to his beloved and reform his character.

The Fairy with Turquoise Hair

The Fairy with Turquoise Hair acts as Alfred's fairy godmother and visits Alfred, Pipì and Ticklythroat in their dreams to give them orders or advice. Before becoming a fairy, she was a beautiful girl called Bella, engaged to be married to Ticklythroat. She appears to Pipì in a dream as a fluffy rabbit with turquoise fur.

Snapper

Snapper is an ancient crocodile who lives in a lake outside the forest of Hullabaloo. He is so old that he has become blind and no longer hunts for food: he just stays still until something falls into his open jaws. He may be a bit decrepit, but he is shrewd, patient and has a wonderful sense of smell. He is not easily tricked, as Pipì painfully finds out.

The Black Monkeys and the Brown Monkeys

During his adventures outside the forest, Pipì chances upon two warring tribes of apes: the Blacks and the Browns. As soon as they see Pipì, they stop fighting and recognize in him the pink monkey that will put an end to all their battles and disagreements. When they appoint him as their emperor, Pipì is at first happy – but he quickly changes his mind when he realizes that with authority comes responsibility, along with some dubious privileges, such as being executed at the end of a fixed term of years. More than anything, Pipì realizes that – with or without an emperor – the two factions are bent on giving each other a bloody nose at the earliest opportunity.

OTHER FAMOUS FICTIONAL APES

Our planet is full of monkeys and apes, real or imaginary, but just like humans, some of them are more famous than others. Here is a selection of some of the most popular fictional simians from the world of literature and films.

King Kong
This giant gorilla has become one of the greatest Hollywood icons of all time. He first appeared in a 1933 film, in which a crew of filmmakers capture him on a small island in the Pacific Ocean and take him to the concrete jungle of Manhattan, with disastrous consequences. The original film was so successful that it spawned countless sequels, remakes, adaptations and spin-offs, including the videogame

Donkey Kong, in which he appears as the villain of the piece, chased and ultimately floored by Mario of Super Mario Bros. fame.

Cheeta

Cheeta is the name of Tarzan's faithful and brave chimpanzee sidekick in the film adaptations of Edgar Rice Burroughs's series of Tarzan novels, written between 1912 and 1947. Funnily enough, in the original novels there is no ape called Cheeta. In later sequels, Burroughs did give Tarzan a simian companion, but this was called Nkima. Another curiosity is that Cheeta was sometimes portrayed in the films as a female and sometimes as a male monkey.

Curious George

This little mischievous monkey could be taken for our Pipì if he didn't have brown fur and was not accompanied on his adventures by a man in a yellow hat and suit (Alfred has much better dress sense). He made his first appearance in a book published in Paris in 1939 under the name of Fifi. Because of the War, his authors – Hans Augusto and Margret Rey, a husband-and-wife Jewish-German couple – had to flee France on self-assembled bicycles and travel first to Spain and then to Portugal and Brazil before settling in the United States. In their baggage they took with them the manuscript of the first *Curious George* book. Many more volumes followed: Hans Augusto would draw the illustrations and Margret would write the stories. George is now one of the greatest celebrity monkeys on the planet.

Planet of the Apes

As we have seen with King Kong, not all monkeys are friendly and kind. *Planet of the Apes* is the name of a celebrated 1968 film based on a novel by the French author Pierre Boulie. In it, some astronauts travel through a time warp and land on a strange planet. They are shocked to find that over 2,000 years have passed since they left, and that the planet they are on is under the control of aggressive, gun-wielding apes who rule over a savage race of humans. They will eventually discover to their dismay that this alien planet is the very earth they had abandoned.

TEST YOURSELF

Have you been keeping an eye on what young Pipì has been up to? Tell us the truth – don't do a Pinocchio on us. And why not also try this multiple-choice quiz to see how attentive you've been? The answers are on p. 107.

1) What does "Pipì" mean in monkey language?
    A) The cheeky one
    B) The prince of disobedience
    C) Smelling like a rose
    D) Coloured like a rose

2) What's the rumbling noise Pipì can hear as he approaches Snapper?
    A) An impending storm
    B) The croc's hungry stomach
    C) A gross gassy frog
    D) Batman's car speeding by

3) What is the name of the kind mouse and billy goat who try to help Pipì out of the sack in which he is imprisoned?
    A) Gnasher and Basher
    B) Nibbler and Fiddler
    C) Nibbler and Basher
    D) Banger and Masher

4) What happens to the robber Ticklythroat when he gets angry?
- A) His head blows off
- B) His limbs stretch out like a shadow
- C) He starts sweating and hyperventilating
- D) He calls his mummy

5) What is the name of Ticklythroat's fellow robbers?
- A) The Swooping Magpies
- B) The Creepy Crows
- C) The Illegal Eagles
- D) The Nimble Nincompoops

6) In which inn do Ticklythroat and Pipì stay for the night?
- A) Beanstalk's Late-Nite Diner
- B) The Midnight Feast
- C) The Cloud Cuckoo Land
- D) The Empty Larder

7) What breed is Alfred's dog?
- A) Chihuahua
- B) Newfoundland
- C) Sausage dog
- D) St Bernard

8) What are the emblems of the two warring monkey generals?

    A) The sun and a full moon
    B) A black crown and a brown crown
    C) A coconut and a conker
    D) A palm headdress and a donkey's skull

9) Where is Pipì made to sleep when he is crowned emperor?
    A) On a heap of feathers
    B) On a hammock
    C) On a bed made of brambles
    D) In a coffin, standing

ANSWERS

1—D
2—B
3—C
4—B
5—A
6—D
7—B
8—D
9—C

SCORES

1 to 3 correct: You really made a monkey out of yourself. **4 to 7 correct:** Not too bad: you'll get a handful of peanuts for dinner. **8 to 9 correct:** Congratulations, you're the top banana!

Brief Glossary of Monkey Language

dop-dops	Candy canes.
glup-glup	Smoking pipe.
Hulla-ba-loo	Hullabaloo, in the Whatchamacallit Forest.
Koo-ra-kah!	It's dinner time!
Kree-kree-pah	We have nothing to give you.
Tatà-ruk Pipì	The rose-coloured monkey has arrived.

ALESSANDRO GALLENZI is the founder of Hesperus Press and Alma Books. His collection of poetry, *Modern Bestiary – Ars Poetastrica*, was published in 2005 to critical acclaim. His satirical novel, *Bestseller*, was published in 2010, followed by *InterRail* in 2012 and *The Tower* in 2014. His verse translation of Alexander Pope's *The Rape of the Lock* won the Premio Biblioteca di Monselice special award in 2010.

Photo: Liam Jackson

AXEL SCHEFFLER was born in Hamburg, Germany. He studied History of Art before moving to the United Kingdom to study illustration at Bath Academy of Art in 1982. Since then he has worked as a freelance illustrator in London. He is best known for the children's books he has illustrated through his partnership with author Julia Donaldson. Together they created *The Gruffalo*, which has sold over ten million copies in almost sixty countries throughout the world. He lives in London.

The Bears' Famous Invasion of Sicily, by Dino Buzzati
illustrated by the author

The Wizard of Oz, by L. Frank Baum
illustrated by Ella Okstad

Lassie Come-Home, by Eric Knight
illustrated by Gary Blythe

Little Women, by Louisa May Alcott
illustrated by Ella Bailey

Black Beauty, by Anna Sewell
illustrated by Paul Howard

The Secret Garden, by Frances Hodgson Burnett
illustrated by Peter Bailey

The Jungle Books, by Rudyard Kipling
illustrated by Ian Beck

Alice's Adventures in Wonderland, by Lewis Carroll
illustrated by John Tenniel

The Railway Children, by E. Nesbit
illustrated by Peter Bailey

What Katy Did, by Susan Coolidge
illustrated by Susan Hellard

The Adventures of Sherlock Holmes, by Arthur Conan Doyle
illustrated by David Mackintosh

For our complete list, please visit:
www.almajunior.com